THROUGH THE SHIMMER

ANANYA SONI

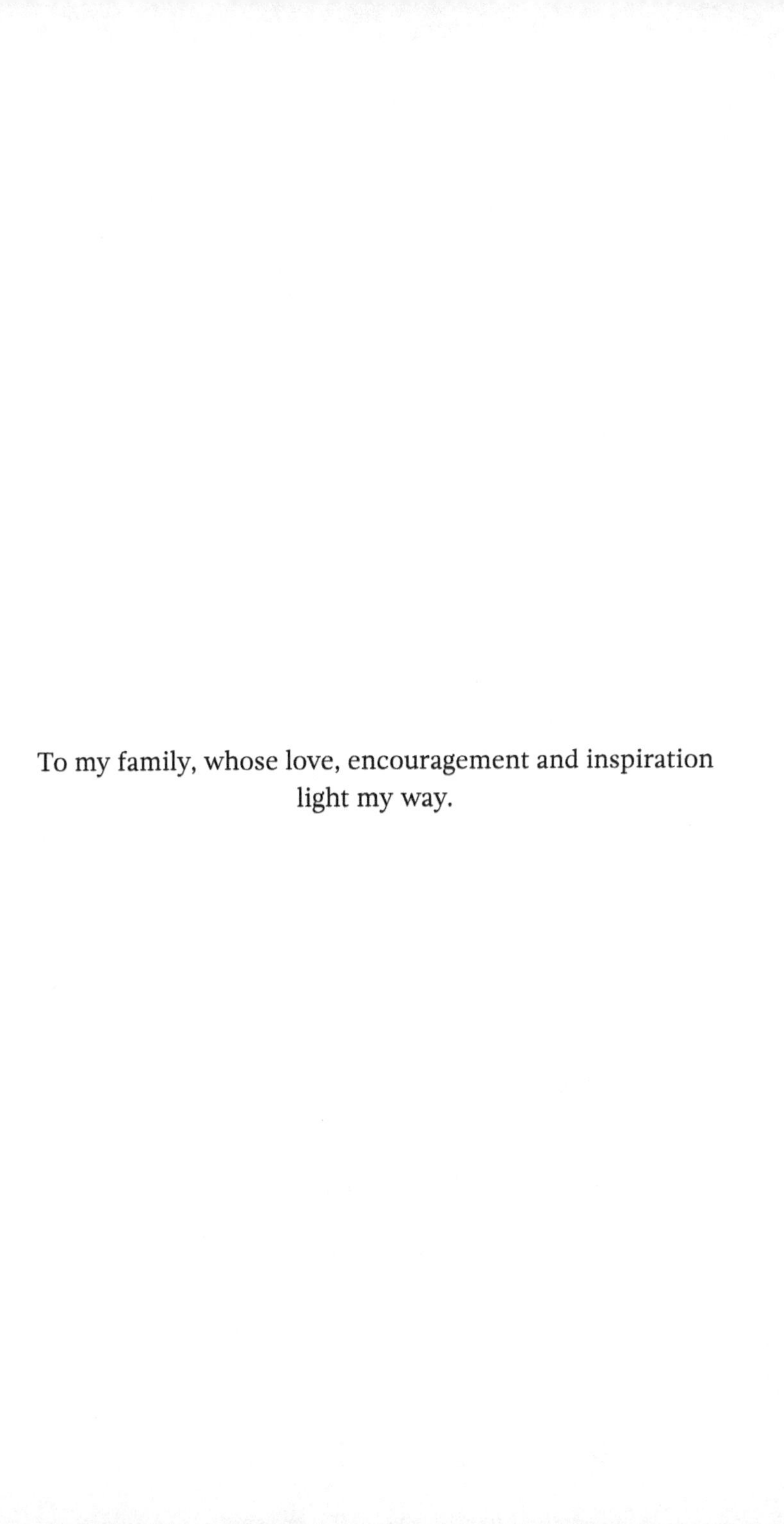

To my family, whose love, encouragement and inspiration
light my way.

Contents

Acknowledgements

Writing this book has been a wonderful journey, and I couldn't have done it alone. I want to thank my family for guiding me every step of the way and inspiring me to write about our adventure together. I am grateful to my teachers and mentors for encouraging me and giving me the opportunity to share my story. Thank you to Notion Press for publishing my book and helping bring my ideas to life.

CHAPTER ONE

THE TRIP TO DUBAI

I'd been counting down the days ever since Mom and Dad told us we were going to Dubai. The week before the trip was a blur of packing and my little brother, Ayansh, constantly asking, "How many more days?" The night before our flight, I was too excited to sleep, imagining all the adventures we'd have.

For once, Ayansh and I actually woke up to the alarm on the first ring and got dressed without anyone nagging us. After a quick breakfast, we hurried to the airport, quickly got through security check-ins, and finally boarded the plane. The flight was filled with the soft chatter of passengers and, of course, Ayansh's endless "Are we there yet?" every few minutes.

When we finally landed, the heat hit us like a wall. The airport buzzed with people from all around the world, everyone rushing somewhere. None of us had any idea just how exciting this trip was about to get. We grabbed our bags, and Dad managed to flag down a taxi. We stuffed our bags inside and headed to our hotel. On the ride, Ayansh pressed his nose to the window, pointing out every palm tree and shiny building we passed.

On our first morning in Dubai, we woke up early, so excited we could hardly stand still. After breakfast, we spent hours at a giant waterpark, plunging down towering slides and lazily floating in the pools. I kept trying to convince Mom to try at least one of the "real" waterslides, but she just laughed and said, "Maybe next time," or, "I'll stick to these gentle ones instead." While swimming, I even found a coin at the bottom of the pool—probably someone's lost souvenir. I kept it, thinking it might bring me luck.

Later, we went to a theme park with rides that twisted and turned high above our heads. I could see the worry on Mom's face as she looked at the roller coasters. Honestly, even I was a little nervous, so we started with the smaller rides. But Dad convinced me to try just one of the big roller coasters, which somehow turned into us riding almost all of them. By the end of the day, my voice was hoarse from all the screaming and laughing.

The next morning, we wandered through Miracle Garden, where flowers stretched in every direction. Mom and I kept stopping to take pictures—there were castles, aeroplanes, and heart-shaped arches made entirely of flowers. Some arrangements looked almost like weird symbols, but I figured it was just my imagination.

That evening, we explored the bustling streets of Global Village. We watched live performances, sampled food from around the world, and browsed the stalls for souvenirs. We even tried Turkish ice cream; the vendor teased Ayansh, refusing to hand over the cone until he was on the verge of tears. It was hilarious to watch. At one point, I thought I heard a whisper behind me, but when I turned, it was just the crowd.

Maybe it was the excitement—or maybe just how tired I was. Either way, it had been a long, unforgettable day.

CHAPTER TWO

THE SHIMMERING PORTAL

The next morning, I woke up with a strange feeling about the day, which I couldn't explain. Perhaps it was the lingering excitement from the previous day or simply the thrill of being somewhere new. After a quick breakfast at the hotel, we set off for IMG Worlds of Adventure, a place we'd all been looking forward to.

As soon as we walked in, I was wowed by the energetic atmosphere—bright lights, superhero music, and people yelling from roller coasters. The place was huge, with different zones themed around Marvel, dinosaurs, and even cartoons. Both Ayansh and I were practically bouncing with excitement, dragging Mom and Dad toward the nearest ride as soon as we got our tickets.

We went on everything we could find: spinning rides that made us dizzy and roller coasters that flipped my stomach. Ayansh kept begging to go on the dinosaur one again, while Mom flat-out refused to try anything that went upside down. Dad, caught between us, ended up going on almost every ride with us.

I was just about to suggest our next stop when I noticed something odd—a faintly glowing shimmer tucked between two attractions, almost hidden behind a Marvel poster. It seemed strange, but I wasn't the type to walk away from a mystery.

"Come look at this, Mom and Dad," I called, trying to figure out what it could be.

Dad looked over. "What is it? Did you find a good ride?"

Ayansh hurried over, eyes wide. "Is it part of the park?" he asked, trying to put his hand through the shimmer.

Mom glanced around and said, "Maybe we should ask someone about it."

But curiosity got the better of us. We stepped closer, and suddenly, everything seemed to ripple and spin. For a split second, the world tilted—and then, just like that, we weren't in IMG Worlds of Adventure anymore.

The sky above us was a canvas of mesmerising pastel hues and rolling meadows stretched across the land. Unicorns, centaurs, pegasuses, griffins, and all kinds of mythical creatures were drinking water from sparkling crystal lakes, and phoenixes soared overhead as if it were the most normal thing in the world. For a moment, we were so stunned that none of us could find our words, our senses amazed by the unreal scene.

"Are we dreaming?" Ayansh said, breaking the silence.

I was too shocked to speak, still trying to process everything that had happened. Slowly, I pinched myself and whispered, "I don't think so."

We stood there, still trying to take in the impossible scene around us. The air felt fresh, with a hint of sweet flowers, which I had never smelled before. The grass beneath us was so soft that I felt as if I were walking on a thick, fluffy carpet. Ayansh was the first to move. He reached down and touched the grass, then looked up at me, eyes wide. "It's real," he whispered. "We're really here."

Mom took a deep breath. "Where are we?" she said softly, glancing around at the landscape.

"Well, wherever we are, we are together, and that's all that matters. Let's see if we can find someone to help us," Dad said.

We started walking, careful not to wander too far from each other. Every step revealed something new: new kinds of flowers, centaurs chatting, and unicorns peacefully grazing. I couldn't help but stare. Everything was just so different!

"This place... It's just like the ones I see in storybooks and have dreamt of visiting my whole life. I just didn't think that it would be so strange," I thought to myself.

"Do you think they have dragons here?" Ayansh yelled, breaking the peaceful silence once again.

"They might, but let's hope they're the friendly kind!" Dad joked.

We had truly stepped into a world beyond our wildest imagination. Still, I couldn't shake the feeling that we were here for a reason. But for now, I decided to enjoy the moment—and stay alert for whatever might come our way.

CHAPTER THREE

MEADOWS AND MAGIC

We wandered through rolling meadows for what felt like hours, marvelling at the mythical creatures we encountered. The sunlight made the grass look golden, and the air smelled fresh and sweet. Suddenly, my eyes landed on an adorable, lost baby unicorn. Her deep blue eyes sparkled brighter than the stars, and I felt an instant connection. There was no way I could leave her behind, not with those pleading puppy eyes. So, I picked her up gently, deciding we'd help her find her mother.

Not long after, Ayansh dashed off toward something. "Ayansh! Don't run off like that—you could get lost!" I called after him. But when I caught up, I froze in amazement. Standing before us was a majestic dragon!

"Wh-what... is that really a dragon?" I stammered.

"Be careful! It might hurt you," I warned, but Ayansh ignored me, reaching out to gently pet the dragon's nose. The dragon lowered its head, clearly enjoying the attention, while Ayansh beamed with excitement. We spent the next half hour bonding with Ayansh's new "pet" dragon.

"Seriously, am I the only one trying to be cautious around here?" I grumbled. My family shot me a knowing look, as if to say, "Look who's talking."

"Okay, okay, but mine was a helpless baby unicorn, not a massive dragon who could eat me for breakfast," I protested.

"You do make a point," my parents said in unison, turning to scold Ayansh for being reckless. I couldn't help but grin to myself. I tried not to look too pleased, but it was fun being right for a change.

We continued our journey, and soon, we found a herd of unicorns grazing by the water. My heart raced with excitement. "We might be able to find Sparkle's mother here!" I exclaimed.

"You gave it a name?" Ayansh scoffed. "Talk about obsessed."

"Hey! Who named his 'pet' dragon Starblaze?" I shot back.

"Ugh, it's just—" Ayansh started, but Mom cut in, "Enough, you two!" I took the chance to slip away and search the herd for Sparkle's mother.

"I'll be back in five!" I called, moving through the unicorns. Sparkle was unique—her ocean-blue eyes and shimmering white coat made her stand out. Just as I was about to give up, I spotted an ethereal unicorn with the same sapphire eyes. I hurried over, and she looked startled at first but relaxed when she saw Sparkle.

"I've come to return someone who belongs to you," I said softly.

"Thank you so much! You have no idea what a favour you've done by bringing my baby back," the unicorn replied, her voice gentle and warm.

I stared in awe. "Y-you can talk?"

"Of course, dear. All mythical creatures here can speak. And for your kindness, if you ever need help, just say my name—Pearl—three times." Before I could say anything more, she vanished into the distance.

I rejoined my family, and we continued through meadows and enchanted forests. After hours of walking (and a few more arguments with Ayansh), we stumbled upon a small, magical village. The air was sweet with the scent of flowers and delicious food. The villagers looked almost human, but each had a magical sparkle in their eyes.

At first, they seemed sceptical, as if expecting trouble. I tried to explain that we meant no harm, even telling them about rescuing Sparkle. Still, they hesitated—until a coin I'd found earlier slipped from my pocket. The moment they saw it, their faces lit up, and they welcomed us warmly. We exchanged confused glances, and I quickly lifted the coin back into my pocket, unaware it was the reason for their sudden change of heart.

They also offered to give us a tour of the village. Of course, we accepted. After having a hearty meal of their native dishes, which left us licking our fingers, we went on a tour of the village with our guide, Lily.

As we wandered around, I noticed that the life there was very similar to that in the real world. I saw people building houses, potters making different kinds of pots with mud, nurses mending people's injuries with their powers, policemen patrolling the streets for thieves, teachers teaching about various topics, and even magizoologists studying the different mythical creatures and jotting down informative notes about them.

I also noticed that their houses were made with the help of a unique woven pattern of vines, twigs, and sticks, along with a special kind of mud that acted like concrete to hold everything together. When I asked Lily more about it, she told me that this special kind of mud could magically keep the house warm or cool, depending on what you wanted. It was amazing to see all the people use their powers to help the village thrive. Their skills were better than anyone I'd ever seen before, and most importantly, they worked together, which was like the cherry on top.

Lily also made us sample some exotic fruits that were specific to only that area of Aetheria, which was supposedly the name of their world. One fruit I tried tasted just like a sweet mango and also gave me the power to float. Then Ayansh tried a fruit that looked like a banana, which gave him invisibility. Mom and Dad refused to try any of the fruits with powers, so they just stuck to the boring ones. Still, they tasted amazing!

After a day full of exploring, we decided to go to bed early. Our rooms were excellent and had little glowing things that looked like stars. And the bed was like sleeping on a cloud; I fell asleep as soon as I lay down.

CHAPTER FOUR

THE VANISHING BOOK

The next morning, when I woke up after a good night's sleep, I couldn't believe the scene outside my window. I rubbed my eyes hard, but I wasn't dreaming! Outside, all the villagers were running from here to there, and the sky, which was once painted in pastel hues, was now being circled by thick, swirling black clouds! The calm world of Aetheria had transformed into a swirl of fear and confusion.

I quickly woke everyone else up, and we rushed outside to find out what had happened. That's when the terrible news struck us. The magical book that powered the whole world's magic—the Liber Magicae—had vanished! This was causing all the magic to spiral out of control! To make matters worse, the thief had cast a powerful curse over the land, forbidding anyone to come in or go out.

We were completely clueless about what to do, so we went straight to the Elders of Aetheria, who were having a heated discussion. "We would like to do anything to help if we can," I began.

No one listened. "Is there something to track the book?" one Elder asked.

"Are you stupid? Of course not; it's a magical book," another replied.

The arguments went back and forth until finally, the leader of the Elders noticed us and asked, "Why are you here, fellow humans?"

"I just wanted to ask if there was anything that we could do to help?" I went on. "I'm sorry—"

"Hey, this happened just after you guys came into our world. Is it you who stole the book?" another interrupted.

"Till now, we didn't even know such a book existed!" I protested.

"Enough!" yelled the Elder. "Anyway, as I was saying—wait! I just realised...you are not from this world, so the curse will not affect you!" he said, his eyes lighting up with hope.

"So are you saying that we are the only ones who can retrieve the book?" I continued.

"Yes, exactly," replied the Elder.

"So it's settled, we will start investigating right away!" shouted Dad.

As we exited the room, I still couldn't take everything in. We, who had entered this world by accident, had now become a part of the crisis the land of Aetheria faced.

CHAPTER FIVE

CLUES IN THE SHADOWS

As we moved out of the Elder building, we decided to split up to make our search easier. My parents headed towards the chamber where the Liber Magicae once rested, and Ayansh and I went out to ask the villagers if they had seen anything unusual. The village air felt tense as if everyone was waiting for answers.

We went to each house we could spot one by one. "Hello, we just came here to ask you if you might have seen anything unusual when the Liber Magicae went missing?" we would ask. Some said, "Sorry, I didn't really spot anything like that." Others said, "Yes, yes, I remember seeing a swift black shadow, sort of. It had a slim figure, so it might have been a girl." Strangely, others who were in the same place at the same time claimed they hadn't noticed anything at all. It was almost as if the truth itself was hiding from us. It seemed odd, but we decided not to dwell on it for now.

One villager named Orla particularly caught my attention. She was keeping to herself and was also present at the crime scene at the exact time the book went missing.

When we asked her the same question, she replied in a nervous tone as if trying to divert suspicion from herself, "Ummmm, no, not really. I didn't see anything." This made me even more suspicious. Her eyes darted to the ground, and she fiddled with the edge of her sleeve. In addition to that, I also heard her muttering something like "keeping secrets." To further confirm my suspicion, I overheard some villagers talking about her previous accusations of theft. Later, I caught a group of elders whispering, "She's always been odd, that one. Never quite fits in."

I couldn't hold back any longer. I went and confronted her about this, and she replied, "I'm very sorry, but I would never do anything to harm my village. The accusations you heard about were misunderstandings among villagers, as I am not much of a social person and prefer to keep to myself." I was still not buying it. "And why should I believe you?"

"I was actually trying to divert suspicion from myself, but I guess I wasn't very good at it because I befriended a forest spirit to meet whom I sneak out at night. This is also why I was there at the crime scene as I was returning from my visit to her. I don't want the villagers to know since everyone has been wary of forest spirits ever since there was some trouble with them ages ago. I didn't want them to suspect me," she replied hesitantly. Her voice trembled, and for a moment, I almost felt sorry for her.

"Wait a minute! Your friend might have seen something the time the book disappeared." As we reached the forest edge, Orla called out, "Oh, Mira... Where are you?" I was astonished. I had never seen anyone so beautiful—her skin shimmered, and her wings were transparent and glittery. She was startled to see us and was about to go back into hiding, but Orla said, "They are not here to harm you, Mira.

They just need help with finding something."

"Were you present here the night the Liber Magicae disappeared?" I started.

"Yes, I was," Mira replied, her voice like the wind rustling through leaves.

"Then, did you see anything that might help us find the thief?"

"Hmm... I saw a cloaked figure, and she dropped a flower, leaving a trail of golden glitter behind her. She also whispered something like highest...peak...highest.....mountains." Mira's wings fluttered anxiously as she spoke, as if recalling the memory made her nervous.

"Thank you so much for your help, Mira. You don't know how big of a favour you have done for us!" I exclaimed, and then Ayansh and I quickly ran to see if that piece of evidence was still there. Unfortunately, the trail of golden glitter was gone, but we did find the flower Mira was talking about. It was delicate, with petals that shimmered silver-blue in the sunlight and a faint trace of golden dust still clung to its stem.

We quickly decided to meet up with Mom and Dad right after to share what we had discovered. As we entered the house, Mom promptly began, "Finally, you guys are here! Can we start?" Everyone nodded.

"So we found something very promising. Near the pedestal, we found a golden feather which couldn't have belonged to any bird in this area. We also found a silver-blue petal nestled in the corner and a faint trail of golden glitter leading away from the pedestal."

"Wait, back it up a little. Was that flower petal like this flower?" I asked, holding up our find.

"Exactly like this one! Where'd you find it?"

"Long story short, Ayansh and I had better luck than you and met a forest spirit who told us that the thief was cloaked and left a trail of golden glitter. Also whispered the words highest...peak...highest...mountains."

"How do you know it isn't lying?" Dad burst out, frowning.

"Because we actually found the flower, but the golden trail was blown away by the strong winds," I replied.

"Okay, so let's start inquiring the villagers about the flower now," Mom commanded. Ayansh and I went to the eastern part of the village while our parents covered the western part. The town was so quiet you could almost hear every step we took.

After another round of inquiries, we met up again. "We had no luck," Dad said sadly.

"But we did!" Ayansh shouted with excitement. "We found out that it is a moon petal, and it grows only high up in the Mysterean Mountains, the highest mountain in the area. Whoever left this behind must have come from there. Now everything clicks together."

"I think we should tell Lily about it and then plan our journey." Excitement buzzed between us as we realised we had our next lead. We all grinned at each other and, almost in unison, shouted, "Off to the Mysterean Mountains we go!" The sense of adventure was back, tinged with a bit of fear. But by then, night had fallen, and the village was quieting down. So, after telling Lily all about it, we decided that it was wiser to leave first thing in the morning.

CHAPTER SIX

SECRETS OF THE MYSTEREAN MOUNTAINS

At dawn, we woke early, hearts pounding with anticipation, ready to begin our journey into the unknown. Dark, ragged clouds covered the sun, making the morning feel more like night.

All the elders and villagers tried to warn us about the dangers that the mountains posed. Still, my family and I were dedicated to helping save the world of Aetheria. One Elder even told me a riddle:

"To open what's hidden, seek what you found,
Not on the earth, but where water surrounds.
Silver and small, it carries your fate,
Place it where secrets linger and voices fade."

He also said that it would help us when the time is right. I didn't think much of it, as the riddle didn't make sense at the time. I tucked it away in my mind, just in case.

Lily even volunteered to come with us on the journey despite the effect the absence of the Liber Magicae had on her. We were very relieved to know that a native Aetherian who knew the ways was going with us. She packed a small satchel with dried moonberries, a glowing lantern, and a tiny vial of sparkling dust "for emergencies," she said.

I was astonished to learn that no one had ever tried to climb those mountains. They had just learnt about it from books and scriptures. This gave me a very uneasy feeling about how this journey would go.

As we began our journey, we noticed that every step closer to the Mysterean Mountains made the weather stranger. The gentle but stormy breeze had suddenly turned into a fierce gust, tugging at our clothes with wild force. It felt as if the mountains themselves were trying to stop us from continuing this journey. We exchanged uneasy glances, but none of us wanted to be the first to suggest turning back. Instead, we pressed on, determined to uncover the truth behind the missing Liber Magicae and the curse that threatened all of Aetheria.

As we finally reached the foot of the mountains, the scene before us left us shaken with terror. The mountains stood so high that they seemed to disappear into the circling black clouds surrounding the peaks. The ground rumbled beneath our feet, and the air was thick with the scent of rain and something ancient. I felt like I had just jumped into a villain movie where the hero doesn't come back trying to save the world. For five minutes, there was utter silence. Not a word from anyone.

"I really don't think I can do this. These mountains should be called the peaks of doom," I thought to myself. My hands were trembling, and I tried to hide it by shoving them in my pockets.

Finally, I gathered the courage to be the first one to step forward. "Is anyone gonna join me?" I said with all the courage I had left in my body. My voice echoed back, sounding much braver than I felt.

As we started trekking in the mountains, I stayed on full alert as if we were out in the open with a murderer on the loose. "Well, the thief could kill us if he or she saw us get in their way. Not the best thought to help my confidence," I thought, and that idea made me shiver. The weather had suddenly become chilly, and we had barely started trekking for ten minutes.

As the path wound higher, the air became thinner and thinner. I noticed that every so often, a silvery mist would roll in, hiding the trail so we could only see a few steps ahead. The mist curled around our ankles, cold and damp, making every shadow look like a lurking creature. I tried to spot a pattern in the way the mist moved, but I couldn't. What I did notice was that whenever I started to feel a little confident, the fog would thicken. Maybe I was just being overly cautious, or maybe it was real. I honestly couldn't tell.

"Why is everyone being so quiet? At home, I couldn't get you to stop talking, Ayansh. Now you've forgotten how to speak?" I joked, trying to lighten the mood.

"We are being careful... You know, so that someone or something doesn't come and stab us in the back," Ayansh countered, his eyes darting nervously to the shadows.

"Okay, Mr. Bravy Brave, then why don't you take the lead?"

"I would, but—"

"Stop it, you two; if we die here, I don't want it to be from hearing you argue," Dad interrupted. "We really need to work together if we are going to do this."

"Yes, Dad," Ayansh and I said in unison. Despite the fear, I felt a flicker of hope. As long as we stuck together, maybe—just maybe—we could do this.

In this manner, we continued to trek for hours, being cautious of anything that might come our way. The mountains seemed to close in around us, their jagged peaks dark against the stormy sky. Every so often, a chill wind would crawl down the slopes, making us shiver and huddle closer together.

"I don't know, but ever since we stepped on those mountains, I felt someone had been eyeing our every move. Maybe it's my illusion, but I am positive that this feeling is true," I thought. The sense of being watched was so strong that I kept glancing over my shoulder, half-expecting to see a pair of glowing eyes in the shadows.

CHAPTER SEVEN

SHADOWS, WHISPERS, AND DOUBT

By now, it was nightfall, and we decided to camp under an old oak tree with strange, twisted branches. I had a bad feeling about it, but we had no choice. It was either that or out in the open. The branches above seemed to twist into shapes, almost like grasping hands, and the wind made them creak and groan.

As we were setting out tents and sleeping bags, I saw a strange shadow behind a tree keeping an eye on us. Now, it couldn't be my imagination so many times. It had to be true now. This trip was definitely making me feel crazy. Just then, I also found the same golden feather we'd seen near the pedestal. That meant we were on the right track! I told everyone the news, and hope once again sparked in the air. Everyone cheered and hooted, excited that we might actually be getting closer.

But as soon as we all took a sip of the tomato soup, the mood crashed. I was almost about to spit it out—it was disgusting.

However, Lily's sparkling dust came in handy. After she sprinkled it in, the dish became delicious. The dust shimmered as it hit the soup, and suddenly, the taste transformed—warm, comforting, with a hint of something magical.

Then, we all went to sleep. I tossed and turned for ages, but I just couldn't stop hearing eerie whispers. They drifted through the branches, sometimes soft and sometimes sharp, as if the wind itself was trying to speak to me.

Finally, just when I managed to fall asleep, I was awakened in the middle of the night by a faint whisper which said, "Leave.........Now.........." As soon as I heard this, I woke up with a start. My heart was pounding in my chest. I sat up and tried to look out of the tent through the small peephole it had. I glanced at my family, who were still fast asleep and wondered if I should wake them. "Had I really heard that, or was it just the wind playing tricks on me? I guess I am being very overcautious on this trip," I thought to myself.

However, I noticed that Lily was not in her sleeping bag. I thought that was strange, especially with the noises. Okay, now I was being paranoid. She might have woken up to get water or something like that. I should just go to sleep.

As I was on the verge of falling asleep, I heard the same whisper louder this time, "Leave now........before it's too late......." Now I was creeped out. I nudged my brother awake. "Did you hear that?" He sleepily shook his head and replied, "Stop it. You're being too sceptical. Just go to sleep. We have a long day tomorrow." But I couldn't sleep now, at all. Because the voice kind of sounded like Lily. I shook my brother again. "I really heard it, and it also sounded like Lily."

"Come on n-" As Ayansh was about to finish his sentence, a cold wind swept through the camp, making the campfire flicker and die. The sudden darkness made every shadow seem alive, and I felt goosebumps rising on my arms.

Seeing this, Ayansh and I quickly woke everyone else up, discussing what we should do. My mother and father were still in sleep mode, and my father even fell asleep amidst the conversation. I had to spray water on their faces to wake them up for a serious discussion.

"I don't think it is safe here for us anymore," I began.

"Oh, you think that it isn't safe for us now? I felt that it wasn't safe for us ever since we stepped on the mountains," Ayansh barked.

"But Lily is with us, and she's helped us so much till now. I'm sure she'll keep us safe," Dad said.

"Yeah, Dad, about that—" As he turned to take Lily's opinion, he discovered she was not in her sleeping bag.

"Where is Lily?" he asked.

"Well, we need to tell you something. So I was woken by a whisper that said, 'Leave... now...' and that was when I noticed that Lily was not in her sleeping bag. Anyway, I decided to ignore it and sleep, but then I heard the whisper louder, and it kind of sounded like Lily," I said.

"Long story short, we think Lily is hiding something and might know something about the missing Liber Magicae."

"Or worse, involved in the book going missing," Ayansh added.

"Come on, guys. If Lily would have been the thief all along, why would she have helped us till now?" Dad countered.

"Uhm...Dad, that is basically how a thief is supposed to behave," I said, trying hard to hold in my chuckle.

"Listen, whether you like it or not, we have to continue this quest and keep an eye out for her," Dad concluded.

"And now let's go to sleep as we have to wake up after 2-3 hours, I guess," Mom added.

The tent felt colder than before, and every rustle outside made my heart race. I lay awake, staring at the canvas above, wondering who I could trust.

CHAPTER EIGHT

PERIL, SHADOWS, AND SURPRISES

The next morning, at dawn, when we were all woken by the sound of birds chirping, I saw that Lily was sleeping peacefully in her sleeping bag. When she woke up, I asked her if she had gone somewhere at night, to which she replied, "No, not really; I actually had an amazing slumber." This seemed very strange and didn't help in proving her innocence. However, it certainly fueled my suspicions about her.

Still, deep down, my heart didn't want to accept the fact that she would actually betray us in such a way. I started coming up with possible reasons; maybe she just needed some fresh air, or maybe she'd gone out to check the path and didn't want us to worry. As we packed up camp, I kept occasionally glancing at Lily. She acted normal, chatting with my mother. But every so often, I caught her eyes flicking to the shadows between the trees, as if she was searching for something—or someone. At this point, I felt my mind was trying to find clues to prove her guilty. But deep down, I hoped she wouldn't betray us like that.

I didn't know what to believe. After another unappetising meal of something, I don't even know what (I just know that it was the worst thing I've ever tasted), we continued our journey. This time, Lily didn't offer to use her magic sparkling dust. I couldn't figure out why. Maybe she was saving it for real emergencies; anyway, who was I to judge? I didn't even know what it was capable of. After about an hour of trekking, we had completed one-third of our journey. To celebrate, we sat on a few rocks, rested, and had some dried moonberries, which were the first real food I'd had on the whole trip to the mountains.

It was then that I noticed something that made my stomach drop—there was golden dust on Lily's clothes! The same kind of dust we'd found near the missing book.

I couldn't believe my eyes! I pulled Mom aside and told her about this.

"Relax, honey. It may be from the use of the sparkling dust at night," Mom said.

"No, Mom, you don't understand. That's the thing. The sparkling dust that we have is silvery-white, not golden. That is the dust that the thief left behind. I'm telling you, she is up to something, and she better have a credible answer for it," I protested. Then I went up to her and said,

"Hey, Lily, I wanna ask you about something-"

"Yeah, yeah, she wants to ask if we can start moving; she wants to finish this journey as soon as possible," Mom interrupted, as usual! And pulled me away from there.

And we continued our journey again! Now, I was watching Lily like a hawk, her every step, just waiting for her to say something wrong that I could use against her. I kept replaying every moment in my head, looking for missed clues.

By now, we had reached the halfway mark of our journey.

"Ooh...Look at this cave. It's so beautiful," my brother said, his voice echoing as he peered into the shadowy entrance.

"Be careful! That place is called the Hollow of Whispers, and it was one of the first places to be formed before Aetheria," Lily warned, her tone suddenly serious.

"So? I don't see why that's a problem," I said, trying to lighten the mood with a grin.

"You didn't let me finish. As a result, that cave has the most unpredictable and wild magic that can also hurt someone seriously if you're not alert," Lily finished, her eyes scanning the darkness. As we passed the cave, I said, "Wow... we really seem to be getting the hang of this. I think we can actually make it after all," feeling a flicker of hope for the first time in a while.

But just as I started to relax, the ground trembled beneath our feet, and a cold wind swept through the gorge, making the hair on my arms stand up.

Right before us was our next obstacle: a rickety bridge stretching across a deep, mist-filled ravine.

"Oof, this bridge has more mold than the 7-day-old bread at home. Am I right, or am I right?" I joked, chuckling, but everyone just stared at me frantically. "Okay, I guess it's a bad time for a joke."

Dad gingerly stepped onto the first plank, which immediately snapped and tumbled into the darkness below. Not knowing what else to do, we decided to take the risk and cross the bridge in single file. But that turned out to be a huge mistake.

The bridge swayed from side to side, ropes creaking, and all of us were hanging on for dear life. Suddenly, out of nowhere, Ayansh slipped and was about to fall into the abyss when I caught his arm. Unfortunately, I also lost my balance, and then Lily grabbed me, pulling me up with surprising strength. Her grip was firm and steady, and for a second, I saw real fear in her eyes—fear for us, not herself.... For a split second, I actually thought she might let go and betray us, but instead, she held on tighter.

Then, randomly, Ayansh whistled—a shrill, clear sound that echoed across the ravine—and suddenly, I remembered, "Pearl, Pearl, Pearl!" I shouted, and to my relief, Pearl appeared in a shimmer of light. And following her was Starblaze, his scales glinting in the thin sunlight.

"When did you teach him that?" I asked Ayansh, still breathless.

"Well, a magician never reveals his secrets," he replied with a wink.

Pearl stepped onto the bridge, her magic glowing silver-blue and weaving around the ropes and planks like living light. Starblaze hovered protectively beside us, his wings stirring the mist.

Pearl's magic strengthened the bridge, and Starblaze took Mom and Ayansh safely to the end.

But the danger did not end there. As Dad safely crossed, weird, snappy vines shot out of the mist and sliced the ropes! Lily and I were falling into the fog when Starblaze swooped underneath and caught us just in time.

"Oh wow, thank you, Starblaze! If you hadn't caught us, we would be vine-meal," I gasped, my heart still pounding. My hands were shaking as I clung to his scales, and I realised that, even with all my doubts, Lily had saved me without hesitation. Maybe, just maybe, I was wrong about her after all.

We were bidding Pearl and Starblaze goodbye when he said, "You all can just travel on my back for the rest of the journey."

"I'm sorry, Starblaze; as tempting as it might sound, we started this on our own, so we need to finish this on our own," I said, my voice tinged with regret.

"Plus, there are some very narrow areas where you might not be able to go," Lily added thoughtfully.

"I understand," Starblaze replied, bowing his head. Pearl and Starblaze both disappeared into the distance, their magic fading into the mist.

"Let's continue our journey, shall we? We have a magic book to retrieve!" I said, trying to sound enthusiastic.

"Alright then!" Everyone replied in unison. Once again, energy and positivity sparked in the air, and everyone was charged up for the journey ahead.

But the threats did not stop there. The air grew colder, and the sky darkened as we continued to climb higher. Every step was harder than the last, and it felt like the mountain itself was testing us. As we drew closer to the peak, it seemed like new challenges were unfolding, and someone—or something—was trying their best to ensure we wouldn't make it there.

Suddenly, right before us stood a pack of wolves, their fur shimmering with frost, their eyes glowing an icy blue.

"Are tho-those wolves?" I stammered, my breath fogging in the cold air.

"Not just any wolves—frost wolves," Lily replied, her voice tense. "Whoever they bite freezes into permanent ice for all of eternity. But they're supposed to be extinct."

"What! So what are they doing here?" I yelled, panic rising in my chest.

"The last of these wolves must be living here in these mountains, guarding the peak. Or maybe someone sent them on purpose," Lily said, stepping in front of us.

"Everyone get behind me!" she called out, her voice steady and commanding.

I was stunned as I watched her face the pack alone. Lily raised her hands, and the air shimmered with the last of her ice powers. The frost wolves snarled but then retreated, spooked by her magic.

I couldn't believe it. She risked her life for our safety. I hugged her so tightly she had to laugh and tell me to loosen up.

"I can't believe you risked your life for us," I said, tears stinging my eyes.

"Well, that's what friends are for, right?" she replied, chuckling.

"Thank you so much. You don't know how grateful I am."

"Come on now, we're only a few metres away from the mountain peak," Lily said, her voice gentle but determined.

As we were just a step away from the peak, I asked everyone, "Are we ready to do this?"

"Yeah!" everyone shouted energetically.

As we stepped onto the mountain peak, I was expecting to see the thief, or a cave, or at least something, but it was deserted—just plain snow and snow everywhere!

"I—I don't understand!" I stuttered. "Where is everything?"

"Hey, maybe it's an illusion or a test, and the book is hidden in the snow," Ayansh suggested, already digging.... We dug through the snow for hours, our fingers numb and spirits sinking.

"We have been digging for hours; I can't believe we did all of this for nothing," I groaned, collapsing onto the snow.

Just as we were about to turn back with heavy hearts, I felt a strange magical pull and suddenly slipped off the edge of the cliff. My life flashed before my eyes as I tumbled, and I heard a whisper in my ear, "Looks like your messenger sold you off." The voice sounded eerily like Lily, but how could that be?

I tried to grab onto a piece of rock, but it broke away in my hand. Just as I thought I wouldn't survive, I felt someone grab me and pull me up. It was Lily. Once again, she had saved my life.

When I scrambled back up, I hugged her tightly, tears of gratitude welling up in my eyes. My parents thanked her, too, their voices shaky with relief.

Now, the suspicions were becoming increasingly painful. "If she was the thief, why did she help me? If not, then why the suspicious behaviour?" I wondered.

CHAPTER NINE

DOWN THE MOUNTAIN, UP WITH SUSPICION

Nonetheless, we started climbing down the mountain, and from the corner of my eye, I thought I saw a black shadow watching us. My heart skipped a beat. The shadow was quick, but for a moment, I was sure it looked just like Lily.

"What? But she's right here with us. How can it be Lily?" I thought, my mind spinning. I looked over at Lily, who was walking next to my mom, talking and laughing like nothing was wrong. Was I just tired and seeing things? Or was something strange really going on?

I tried to brush it off, but the weird feeling stayed with me. Every time I glanced back, I couldn't shake the thought that someone—or something—was still watching us from the shadows.

Now, all of us were excruciatingly tired, and we decided to call Pearl and Starblaze. When they reached us, I quickly jumped on Pearl's back and leaned on her soft mane.

"Wow, you sure are tired," she joked, her voice warm and musical.

I nodded, too exhausted to even speak.

Ayansh, somehow still full of energy, grinned and said, "Let's have a race! You and Lily on Pearl, and me, Mom, and Dad on Starblaze."

Pearl and Starblaze exchanged competitive glances, their eyes sparkling. By that time, I had already fallen asleep, completely clueless about everything.

"Okay, On your marks, get set, go!" Mom shouted.

Starblaze raced off, flapping his wings as fast as he could, while Pearl conjured a magic bridge and sprinted away. To everyone's surprise, both reached the village at the same time.

As we entered the village with empty hands, the smiles on the villagers' faces disappeared. Everyone stopped cheering and was too stunned to speak. The town was dead silent.

"Wh-Where's the book?" one person finally asked.

"It turns out that all of it was just a wild goose chase," we replied, embarrassed.

As we were heading to our house through the crowd, something extraordinary happened. The Liber Magicae appeared in front of me, hovering in the air, glowing faintly.

Everyone's frowns turned upside down, and they started cheering and hooting.

"We knew you were joking!" the crowd shouted.

"But we—" I tried to explain, but they didn't let me finish.

My parents looked at me, confused. "Where'd you find this? Why didn't you tell us?" Mom and Dad asked.

"That's the thing, I didn't find it. How come it just appeared?" I replied, worry creeping into my voice.

"Come on, the important thing is that the problem is solved. Just enjoy the moment," Mom said, but I couldn't shake the feeling that something was wrong.

I quickly ran to the Elders' building and told them about this.

"Hmmmm...That is strange," the chief Elder replied, stroking his beard. "Well, there is a test to verify the authenticity of the magic book. You might be surprised, but this is not the first time such a thing has happened."

"Really? So, you mean that the Liber Magicae has been stolen more than once? When and by whom?" I pressed.

"Well, I don't have the liberty to say. All you should know is that a similar thing happened, and since then, we have invented a magical test which can tell whether the book is real or not."

"So shall we start with it?" I asked impatiently.

"Sure, let's begin. For that, we need to gather around the old oak tree in a circle around the book, holding hands. Each person will ask a question to the book regarding the history of Aetheria or any other topic they desire, which only the true book can answer. If it succeeds, then it is the true book; if it fails to do so, then it is a fake."

One by one, each Elder went and asked a question to the book, and surprisingly, it seemed to answer correctly!

"Which was the first spell ever cast in Aetheria?" The book's pages fluttered, and glowing letters formed: "The Spell of Awakening, said by Elder Mage."

"What is the oldest Law of Magic?" New words appeared in the book: "Balance, for every spark of magic, a shadow falls. For every hero, there is a villain."

Now, it was finally my turn, and I knew what to ask.

"What is the true purpose of the coin I found?"

"The coin is a Token of Remembrance. It will glow softly to warn you of danger, shield you from minor harm, and serve as a keepsake to remember Aetheria by when your journey ends."

I was a bit surprised by its answer, as the coin did not really glow to warn us of danger in the mountains, but I figured we must not have noticed it.

When all the other Elders finished, the chief Elder concluded, "We can safely say that this is the real Liber Magicae, as it answered all our questions correctly."

I seemed genuinely satisfied and even ran to tell the rest of the villagers about it, but deep down, I still had my doubts.

They set up a massive celebration in honour of this, with delicious food, music, and games. One thing seemed weird: the weather had still not improved, even though the book was back. When I went to my parents about this, they just said, "Maybe it's just a bad weather day. Come on, now it is also proven that it is the real book; let's enjoy the party."

I smiled and walked away from there, saying I had some work to do.

But I couldn't let it go. The weather in Aetheria was never supposed to be bad—Lily had told me that herself. All the pieces just weren't fitting together yet.

CHAPTER TEN

TRUTHS AND SECOND CHANCES

I went to the Liber Magicae to do some investigating, but I hadn't ever seen the real book to spot any differences. Just as I turned back and was about to walk out of the chamber, I heard someone whisper my name, "Ananya... Ananya..."

I spun around, my heart pounding. The chamber was empty, but the whisper came again, soft and urgent: "Ananya..."

"Who is it? What do you want?" I called out, trying to sound braver than I felt. The whispering didn't stop. I was about to ignore it and go when I saw that the book was glowing faintly. A strange shiver ran down my spine.

"Have you been whispering my name?" I asked, almost expecting an answer. Curiosity got the better of me, so I reached out and touched the cover. Instantly, a surge of magic pulled me into a vision!

There, I saw someone who looked exactly like Lily, being banished from Aetheria! My eyes widened. She had

Lily's face, but her eyes were colder, and a sly, mischievous smirk played across her face. However, it didn't reveal why she was being banished, just that the chief of Elders was the one sending her away.

My mind raced. Was this what the Elder meant by this has happened more than once? Did she steal the book last time, too? So many questions were storming my mind. I felt very confused. I think it was Lily's twin. But why hadn't Lily ever mentioned having a twin? Was she hiding something, or was she just ashamed?

But the story continued. After being banished, when she had nowhere else to go, she kept wandering and wandering in the far part of Aetheria until she received a warning that a greater threat was coming for Aetheria. So she stole the book—maybe not to hurt Aetheria, but to protect it. But the vision didn't show her putting a curse on the land. Perhaps something else is out there, from which Lily's twin tried to protect the book. Maybe she's misunderstood, and to divert suspicion from herself, she framed Lily.

I felt so bad. All this time, she was just thinking the best for me, and I blamed her for something so cruel!

Just then, I noticed something glowing in the background. It was the Liber Magicae! That means the one in the village is a fake! I was right. All my instincts were right!

As the vision ended, I was pulled back into the chamber before I could ask any questions, fading with a soft whisper, "Everything is not how it seems. Magic is born where hearts meet."

I felt terrible for doubting Lily. I needed to apologise to her right away. However, first, I needed to tell my family that the real Liber Magicae is still out there.

I quickly ran to where the celebration was taking place and pulled my family and Lily aside.

"Guys, I just found out something, but first, I need to apologise to Lily."

"I'm very, very sorry for suspecting you as the thief, Lily. You know, with all the clues and all, I got a little carried away. You always wished the best for me and my family, and I took your intentions in the wrong way. I hope you can forgive me," I said in an apologetic tone.

"I understand. It might be very hard for you and your family to be the only ones who can help, and it's a lot of pressure. You were just checking out all the possibilities," she replied, opening her arms for a hug.

"Thank you so much," I whispered as I hugged her. Soft shimmers appeared in the room, swirling around us.

"Okay now, Ananya, did you see anything that might help us reach the book in the vision?" Mom asked.

"Yes, I saw Lily's twin go into a chamber and place the book. It seemed familiar, but I couldn't exactly recognise it," I replied.

"Well, try your best, as the vision is our only hope of finding the book," Mom encouraged.

After thinking for a while, like five minutes, I finally recognised the place.

"The Hollow of Whispers! That's it! It was the Hollow of Whispers," I yelled with excitement, even though it was not something exciting.

Lily's eyes widened. "A-Are you sure it was the Hollow of Whispers? Describe it to me," she said, her voice trembling.

"It was a dark cave, with swirls of random magic floating around and eerie whispers," I described.

"Okay, it is the Hollow of Whispers," she confirmed, a hint of terror in her voice.

"We needed to plan our next move very carefully and be on high alert, as the Hollow of Whispers is the most dangerous place in Aetheria. Let's discuss this with the Elders. Maybe they can help us." Lily said in a tense voice.

"Wait, so you mean to say that we have to climb the mountain once again?" Ayansh yelled, groaning.

"Guess we'll find out," Lily added.

And we went to the Elders to tell them about everything.

"Very intriguing; there is a secret passage that will directly lead you to the Hollow of Whispers on the far side of the Mysterean Mountains," the chief Elder said.

I noticed Lily's face go pale as he mentioned the far side of the mountains. They described the path to us, and we thanked them for their help. As we were leaving the building, I asked Lily, "Why did you go pale as he mentioned the far side of the mountains?"

"That part of the mountains is bizarre. Creepy things happen there, like walking trees and other inanimate objects acting like they are alive," Lily replied, trembling.

"Come on! We've already faced so many challenges. What's a few walking trees compared to all that? We can do this together," I said, trying to encourage her.

"Let's leave first thing in the morning then," she replied, sounding a bit more confident.

"So we should start packing," I added.

And we went into our house and began packing our bags. My family packed some of the leftover snacks from home while Lily packed the actual essentials in her small satchel: dried moonberries, a little sparkling dust, and a glowing lantern.

As night fell, we all went to bed early to recharge for the big day we had ahead of us.

CHAPTER ELEVEN

THE HOLLOW'S SECRET

At dawn, when I was woken up by the sound of chirping, I looked at the time and quickly woke everyone up. "Come on, guys, wake up; we have to leave for the Hollow of Whispers." Slowly, the rest of my family woke up groaning.

"Seriously, I was in the middle of an amazing dream," Ayansh grumbled sleepily.

"Yeah, well, saving Aetheria is more important than your dream," I teased, rolling my eyes.

We all freshened up and got ready for our trip, stuffing our bags with snacks, water, and anything else we thought we might need. By that time, Lily was already standing in front of our door.

"Good morning, everyone!" she greeted us as I opened the door and let her in.

"Wow, you sure are an early bird," Mom joked.

"Yes, I sure am!" Lily giggled, her energy making the rest of us smile despite our tiredness.

Soon, we set off, determined to finish this once and for all. When we came nearer to the far side of the mountains, I noticed some really peculiar things. Lily wasn't wrong when she said that side was creepy. All the inanimate objects seemed almost possessed. I felt terrified while passing through there. Bushes rustled, and trees seemed to move on their own, even though there was no wind. At first, I thought they wouldn't bother me, but the way they shifted and creaked made my heart pound and sent chills down my spine.

"It honestly felt like my soul was about to jump out of my body. Just ignore them and keep walking straight," Lily advised. "If they feel you aren't interested, they won't do anything."

Finally, after what felt like an eternity, we arrived at a place that resembled a tunnel leading upward.

"Guys, this must be it! This must be what the Elder was talking about." I said enthusiastically.

We all stood there for a minute, staring at the entrance, waiting for someone to take the lead. Finally, when no one stepped forward, Lily took a deep breath and started moving upwards in the tunnel. We all followed one by one. The tunnel was steep, and we had to be careful not to slip.

While climbing up, several questions crossed my mind. "If Lily's twin hid the book here, then why didn't she put someone on guard? What if the vision was just another trick of hers, and the book was actually somewhere else entirely? I guess we'll find out soon," I wondered.

After a long climb through the slippery, wet tunnel, we reached a place which looked like a chamber. The air felt cold and damp, and there were random swirls of magic just floating around. Shadows danced across the walls, and I could also hear eerie whispers, chanting weird secrets of the past, but I didn't pay much attention.

"Empty? Again?" I groaned.

"Come on now, I think Lily's twin would be smart enough to not place the Liber Magicae right in front of us. She would have needed to put in effort to hide it," Mom explained.

"Alright then, let's look for it carefully. I'll examine this side. Lily, you go there, Ayansh there, and Mom and Dad, you can go in that area," I said, and all of us began examining the cave as if our lives depended on it. Well, it kind of did.

Suddenly, out of nowhere, I heard whispers that sounded like my own voice but twisted and mean. "You're not really brave enough for this. You'll never find the real book. Your family only made it this far because of luck, not you." I tried to ignore them, but then another voice joined in—a softer, sadder version of my own. For a moment, I felt as though invisible walls had emerged, separating me from my family.

"Why did you ever suspect Lily? She was your friend. They're all counting on you, but you're going to fail." A chill ran down my spine. For a moment, I felt the cave walls closing in on me, the whispers making me drown in my thoughts. "Is this true? Well, until a few days ago, I was just a normal girl living an ordinary life. I guess I'm really not cut out for this," I started thinking. "Maybe I will never be able to find the book. I'm just leading my family into a trap."

I took a deep breath. "Wait a second, these whispers are just trying to distract me so that I wouldn't be able to find the book. That means it must really be here! I should just ignore them and focus on what's really important," I told myself.

"Why keep searching? You'll only fail again. Go home, Ananya. This isn't your story to finish."

I clenched my fists, trying to block out the voices, but they only grew louder, echoing every doubt I'd ever had. "Go away! You aren't real; what you're saying isn't true, and I'll show you," I yelled in my mind.

Suddenly, I heard Mom's voice, faint but real. "Ananya, Ananya, what were you thinking about?"

"Nothing, Mom. Did you find anything yet?" I replied in a relieved tone.

As I searched the swirling, whispering chamber, my eyes caught a sparkle of gold near the far wall. I ran over, bent down, and picked up a golden feather.

"Look!" I called to the others. "It's just like the feather we found at the start."

Lily's eyes widened. "That's a sign," she whispered. "It means we're close."

CHAPTER TWELVE

BREAKING THE BARRIER

After what felt like forever, I noticed something strange. Hanging in the middle of the air was a hole—not a keyhole, but a thin, small hole. I stared at it, confused. "What could fit in there?" I wondered aloud.

Just then, I remembered a riddle that an Elder told us previously.

"To open what's hidden, seek what you found,
Not on the earth, but where water surrounds.
Silver and small, it carries your fate,
Place it where secrets linger and voices fade."

Suddenly, it all clicked. "To open what's hidden" must mean the place where the Liber Magicae is. "Seek what you found, not on the earth, but where water surrounds." What did I find in a water body? The coin! "Silver and small, it carries your fate"—that definitely describes the coin I found at the waterpark. "Place it where secrets linger and voices fade"—that has to be the Hollow of Whispers!

"Hey guys! Look at this hole," I called out to everyone. "Remember the riddle the Elder told us? I think it's about the coin I found at the waterpark. Maybe I'm supposed to put it in here. Should I try it?"

Ayansh peered over my shoulder, eyes wide. "Go for it. If it's a trap, at least it'll be an interesting one," he joked, trying to sound brave but clearly nervous.

Everyone else gave me encouraging nods and reassuring smiles.

I took a deep breath and slid the coin into the hole. For a moment, nothing happened. I felt my heart sink. "What if those whispers were right? What if I really can't do this?" I thought, doubt creeping in. Just as I turned back, a door to the chamber slid open out of thin air.

There it was—the real Liber Magicae—floating in the middle of a dark, endless room, surrounded by swirling magic. I reached out to grab it, but as soon as my fingers touched the cover, the book vanished and reappeared behind me. I tried again, and the same thing happened, over and over, as if the book was playing some kind of magical game.

"Now, even the coin is gone. What can we do?" I asked everyone.

"Wait a second! Don't you remember?" Lily said suddenly. "When I forgave you, soft shimmers appeared in the room, and when you and Ayansh argued, the weather got worse, but when you made up, flowers bloomed in our path."

"And at the end of my vision, I heard a whisper, 'Magic is born where hearts meet.' " I added, recalling the memory.

"Unity! Unity is the key to unlocking this!" Lily exclaimed.

"Let's all place our hands on there together," I said quickly. We all reached out and placed our hands on the swirling magic at the same time. I whispered, "Together." Instantly, the barrier disappeared! We all cheered and hugged each other, overjoyed.

"This is finally over! Let's take this back to the village and share the good news." I beamed.

We picked up the book and started climbing down the tunnel. "If the tunnel is so steep and slippery, then why don't we slide down instead," Ayansh suggested.

"Good idea!" We shouted in unison, and all of us came sliding down, laughing the whole way.

"I don't think I can take walking through that forest again," I said, terrified. The memory of those moving trees and bushes made me shudder.

"You know what that means," I yelled. "Pearl, Pearl, Pearl!" At the same time, Ayansh whistled loudly. We completed the journey on their backs. I also shared the good news with them, "Look at this, we finally found the book!"

"That's great!" they both replied in unison.

As we soared above the treetops, I felt a huge weight lift from my shoulders. The real Liber Magicae was finally safe in my hands, and it seemed like everything we'd worked for had finally paid off.

CHAPTER THIRTEEN

THE POWER OF UNITY

And as we landed in the village, smiles once again ran across the villagers' faces. I handed the book back to the chief of Elders, and he took it to the empty pedestal. We followed him, and as soon as he kept the book on the pedestal—nothing happened!

"What could be wrong this time?" I groaned again!

"Maybe the weather is bad because of the curse put on Aetheria, not because of the book's absence," Lily suggested.

"Maybe. But now, what will break this curse?" I wondered aloud, watching as dark clouds continued to swirl overhead.

The Elders tried many rituals, calling on ancestors and making offerings, but nothing seemed to work. Then suddenly, arguments arose between the villagers.

"See, I told you this can never work," one yelled.

"Oh yeah! Like what you suggested worked?" another yelled in reply.

I watched the sky grow even darker with each angry word and lightning flash between the clouds with every shout. "Maybe unity is the key to this, too," I thought.

"Everyone, please hold hands and form a circle around the book," I yelled.

"What are you doing?" an Elder whispered to me with uncertainty.

"Trust me. Plus, what do we have to lose?" I replied.

As everyone formed the circle, I told them, "It's not the magic that's broken—it's us. We're so focused on our differences and disagreements that we forget about all the good times we've shared. Magic can't return if we keep arguing. We need to work together if we want to see the clear sky again. So, one by one, let's each say something nice about someone or apologise to a person we've argued with."

Some agreed, nodding while others crossed their arms and muttered things like, "Like this kid's idea will work," and, "I would never apologise to him again." But I started anyway.

"I want to sincerely apologise to Lira for thinking she might have been the thief. I couldn't have been more wrong. She is the sweetest and kindest person I have ever met. Thank you for everything."

As I spoke, something amazing happened—the book began to glow faintly, and I noticed the clouds overhead thin slightly. One by one, as we spoke, the book shone a little brighter, and the thick black clouds became lighter. Even those who were initially reluctant to talk and made comments now wanted to apologise voluntarily.

As the last person spoke, a bright light came from the book, and the curse was lifted! The sky was once again painted with shimmering pastels, and beautiful flowers bloomed. The lands were once again roamed by mighty mythical creatures, and the charm of Aetheria returned.

CHAPTER FOURTEEN

FAREWELL, AETHERIA

We all cheered in happiness.

"We could not ever repay you for the help you did. We would like you to stay in Aetheria for a few days and explore it. Also, we will have a grand celebration to honour you today, so be prepared!" the Chief Elder announced.

"Of course, we would love to stay," I replied for all of us, my heart filled with excitement.

We hurried to our house to get ready for the grand celebration. But even as I smiled and joined in the preparations, questions kept swirling in my mind. Why did all the clues, whispers, and visions only come to me? Why not anyone else? And why was Lily never affected by the absence of the book or the curse on the mountains? The vision never showed Lily's twin actually putting a curse on the land—so was there even a curse, or was something else at play? Maybe some mysteries are never meant to be solved.

So, for the rest of my time in Aetheria, I decided to let go of my worries and savour every moment.

That night, the celebration was full of mouthwatering dishes, music, and endless fun! Over the next few days, we explored more of the land. I visited Pearl and Sparkle to see how they were doing, and Ayansh went to meet Starblaze. We also went on a safari ride through the meadows, where I made new friends and soaked in the natural beauty.

"This world was so peaceful; I wish I could stay here forever, in the magical lands of Aetheria," I would think. But then I'd remember about my grandparents waiting for me at home, and I knew I couldn't stay forever.

We also visited ancient ruins, learning about the history of Aetheria—how it was formed, who created it, and so much more. I can honestly say those days in Aetheria were one of the best of my life.

But, like all good things, our adventure had to come to an end. When it was time for us to go back to Dubai, I felt emotional. I didn't want to leave Lily and all the fantastic people I had met.

The Elders gave me a golden pendant with a sparkling star charm so I could always carry a piece of Aetheria with me. I hugged Lily tightly before leaving and said, "Maybe we'll meet again someday."

As we were about to leave Aetheria and go through the portal, I heard a familiar whisper: "Some adventures don't end so soon."

Back in Dubai, I kept thinking about that whisper, certain that Aetheria wasn't truly gone from my life. For now, we had our everyday lives to return to—but I knew I'd always carry a little magic with me wherever I went.